Snake Charmer

Kelly Doudna

Illustrated by C. A. Nobens

Consulting Editor, Diane Craig, M.A./Reading Specialist

ABDO
Publishing Company

Published by ABDO Publishing Company, 4940 Viking Drive, Edina, Minnesota 55435.

Printed in the United States.

Credits
Edited by: Pam Price
Curriculum Coordinator: Nancy Tuminelly
Cover and Interior Design and Production: Mighty Media
Photo Credits: Yoke Liang Tan/BigStockPhoto.com, Digital Vision, iStockphoto/Brandon Alms, iStockphoto/Daniel Halvorson, Jupiterimages Corporation, Jeff LeClere, Photodisc, ShutterStock

Library of Congress Cataloging-in-Publication Data

Doudna, Kelly, 1963-
    Snake charmer / Kelly Doudna; illustrated by Cheryl Ann Nobens.
        p. cm. -- (Fact & fiction. Critter chronicles)
    Summary: Charlie Charmer, the new rattlesnake in school, attracts the attention of fellow slithery classmate Rose Hognose. Alternating pages provide facts about snakes.
    ISBN 10 1-59928-470-7 (hardcover)
    ISBN 10 1-59928-471-5 (paperback)

    ISBN 13 978-1-59928-470-5 (hardcover)
    ISBN 13 978-1-59928-471-2 (paperback)
    [1. Snakes--Fiction.] I. Nobens, C. A., ill. II. Title. III. Series.

PZ7.D74425Sn 2006
[E]--dc22

                                                                                    2006005704

SandCastle Level: Fluent

SandCastle™ books are created by a professional team of educators, reading specialists, and content developers around five essential components—phonemic awareness, phonics, vocabulary, text comprehension, and fluency—to assist young readers as they develop reading skills and strategies and increase their general knowledge. All books are written, reviewed, and leveled for guided reading, early reading intervention, and Accelerated Reader® programs for use in shared, guided, and independent reading and writing activities to support a balanced approach to literacy instruction. The SandCastle™ series has four levels that correspond to early literacy development. The levels help teachers and parents select appropriate books for young readers.

Emerging Readers
(no flags)

Beginning Readers
(1 flag)

Transitional Readers
(2 flags)

Fluent Readers
(3 flags)

These levels are meant only as a guide. All levels are subject to change.

FACT & FICTION

This series provides early fluent readers the opportunity to develop reading comprehension strategies and increase fluency. These books are appropriate for guided, shared, and independent reading.

FACT The left-hand pages incorporate realistic photographs to enhance readers' understanding of informational text.

FICTION The right-hand pages engage readers with an entertaining, narrative story that is supported by whimsical illustrations.

The Fact and Fiction pages can be read separately to improve comprehension through questioning, predicting, making inferences, and summarizing. They can also be read side-by-side, in spreads, which encourages students to explore and examine different writing styles.

FACT OR FICTION? This fun quiz helps reinforce students' understanding of what is real and not real.

SPEED READ The text-only version of each section includes word-count rulers for fluency practice and assessment.

GLOSSARY Higher-level vocabulary and concepts are defined in the glossary.

SandCastle™ would like to hear from you.

Tell us your stories about reading this book. What was your favorite page? Was there something hard that you needed help with? Share the ups and downs of learning to read. To get posted on the ABDO Publishing Company Web site, send us an e-mail at:

sandcastle@abdopublishing.com

Snake charmers appear to hypnotize snakes, but the snakes are just following movements of the charmers as they play their instruments.

Charlie Charmer is the new rattlesnake in school. All the girls make goo-goo eyes when they see him.

Snakes' hearts can move around to allow the passage of swallowed prey.

Rose Hognose and Scarlet King stand by their lockers. Charlie slithers down the hall toward them.

"He's so cute!" Rose exclaims, her heart pounding. "I wish he'd ask me out on a date."

7

Rattlesnakes add a new segment to their tails each time they shed their skin.

Scarlet says, "Listen! You can hear his rattling from here."

Rose checks herself in her locker mirror. "Do I look okay, Scarlet?" she asks.

9

Snakes smell by flicking their tongues. This brings air inside their mouths to an organ that detects odors.

Rose whispers, "Shh! Here he is!" In a louder voice, she says, "Hi, Charlie."

Charlie replies, "Hi, Rose. Your perfume smells nice."

11

Hognose snakes will roll over and play
dead to trick predators.

Rose is so excited
that all she can
say is, "Oh thanks,
Charlie!" before
she faints.

Snakes don't have external ears. Instead, ground vibrations reach the inner ear through the lower jawbone. This helps snakes determine the size and location of nearby animals.

When Rose wakes up, Scarlet says, "Come on, Rose, it's lunchtime. You'll feel better if you eat something." Rose and Scarlet head for the lunchroom.

Rose says, "Charlie's going to sit with us. I can just feel it!"

Snakes shed their skin. Young snakes shed more often than adults because they are growing rapidly.

When Charlie comes through the line, sure enough, he walks toward Scarlet and Rose. He says, "Hi, girls. Mind if I sit with you?" Charlie doesn't wait for an answer. He takes off his jacket and throws it onto the back of a chair at their table.

17

Medium- and large-sized snakes can eat up to nine pounds of rodents per year.

Charlie asks, "Rose, what are you doing Friday night? Would you like to go out for a burger and a malt and then to the dance?"

Rose almost faints again. "I'd love to, Charlie," she says. "It's a date!"

19

FACT OR FICTION?

Read each statement below. Then decide whether it's from the FACT section or the FICTION section!

1. Rattlesnakes add a new segment to their tails each time they shed their skin.

2. Snakes wear perfume.

3. Hognose snakes will roll over and play dead to elude predators.

4. Snakes wear jackets.

ANSWERS
1. fact 2. fiction 3. fact 4. fiction

Snake charmers appear to hypnotize snakes, but the 8
snakes are just following movements of the charmers 16
as they play their instruments. 21

Snakes' hearts can move around to allow the 29
passage of swallowed prey. 33

Rattlesnakes add a new segment to their tails each 42
time they shed their skin. 47

Snakes smell by flicking their tongues. This brings 55
air inside their mouths to an organ that detects odors. 65

Hognose snakes will roll over and play dead to trick 75
predators. 76

Snakes don't have external ears. Instead, ground 83
vibrations reach the inner ear through the lower 91
jawbone. This helps snakes determine the size and 99
location of nearby animals. 103

Snakes shed their skin. Young snakes shed more 111
often than adults because they are growing rapidly. 119

Medium- and large-sized snakes can eat up to nine 129
pounds of rodents per year. 134

Charlie Charmer is the new rattlesnake in school. All the girls make goo-goo eyes when they see him.

Rose Hognose and Scarlet King stand by their lockers. Charlie slithers down the hall toward them.

"He's so cute!" Rose exclaims, her heart pounding. "I wish he'd ask me out on a date."

Scarlet says, "Listen! You can hear his rattling from here."

Rose checks herself in her locker mirror. "Do I look okay, Scarlet?" she asks.

Rose whispers, "Shh! Here he is!" In a louder voice, she says, "Hi, Charlie."

Charlie replies, "Hi, Rose. Your perfume smells nice."

Rose is so excited that all she can say is, "Oh thanks, Charlie!" before she faints.

7
16
19
27
34
35
42
52
60
62
71
76
85
90
97
98
109
114

When Rose wakes up, Scarlet says, "Come on, Rose, it's lunchtime. You'll feel better if you eat something." Rose and Scarlet head for the lunchroom.

Rose says, "Charlie's going to sit with us. I can just feel it!"

When Charlie comes through the line, sure enough, he walks toward Scarlet and Rose. He says, "Hi, girls. Mind if I sit with you?" Charlie doesn't wait for an answer. He takes off his jacket and throws it onto the back of a chair at their table.

Charlie asks, "Rose, what are you doing Friday night? Would you like to go out for a burger and a malt and then to the dance?"

Rose almost faints again. "I'd love to, Charlie," she says. "It's a date!"

122
131
138
139
149
152
159
168
178
188
199
207
219
225
233
238

GLOSSARY

elude. to avoid or escape from

goo-goo eyes. looking at someone with a foolish, love-struck expression

hypnotize. to cause to enter a sleeplike state

malt. short for malted milk, a mixture of powdered milk and sprouted barley blended with ice cream and flavoring

odor. scent

predator. an animal that hunts others

segment. a section or part of something

slither. to slip and slide like a snake